Summer Dreams

Summer has long been the favourite season for children.

Summer means warm days, playing outdoors with friends

and family, playing summer sports – and school is out!

Summer is a time when children are free to play,

explore – and just have fun.

First published in Canada in 2004 by
McArthur & Company
322 King St. West, Suite 402
Toronto, Ontario
M5V 1J2
www.mcarthur-co.com

National Library of Canada Cataloguing in Publication

Newby, John, 1940–
    Summer Dreams / John Newby.

ISBN 1-55278-419-3

    1. Summer—Pictorial works—Juvenile literature. 2. Amusements—Pictorial works—Juvenile literature. I. Title.

PS8577.E778S95 2004   j790.1   C2004-900848-X

Cover and interior design by Counterpunch/Peter Ross
Printed and bound in Canada by Friesens

The publisher would like to acknowledge the financial support of the Government of Canada through the Book Publishing Industry Development Program, the Canada Council for the Arts, and the Ontario Arts Council for our publishing activities. We also acknowledge the Government of Ontario through the Ontario Media Development Corporation Ontario Book Initiative.

10 9 8 7 6 5 4 3 2 1

SUMMER DREAMS

John Newby

McArthur & Company

Toronto

Summer days start slowly.

Fresh breezes stir new leaves.

The whole world is out there to explore.

Curious children, busy ladybug –

a wet nose touches a wary turtle.

Summer air is warm and still.

In a meadow dotted with buttercups,

friendships are made with a quiet touch.

Silent friends, forever.

The goalkeeper's job is important.

Watching and waiting,

ready to spring into action –

as the last defence.

Summer rookie swings her bat.

She's the youngest player of all,

with too-big socks on short legs,

wondering if she can remember all the rules.

Summer heroes come in all sizes.

Big brother remembers how far away the basket used to seem.

Big sister shares magical secrets.

Summer minds take flight.

There's all the time in the world
to dream of being different for a day.

Countless happy hours
imagining with Grandma and friends.

Summer friends meet on the field.

With lots of ways to pass the time,
until it's your turn to play.

Summer days at the beach are the best.

Hey, that tower is crooked!

(There's always a critic.)

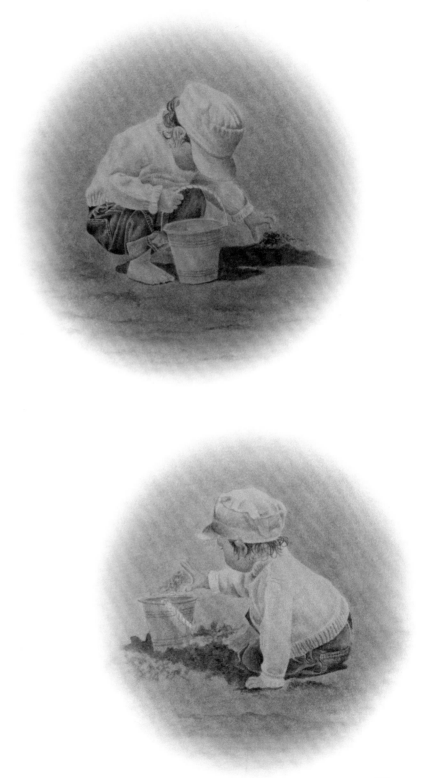

Summer skills are handed down.

Grandpa knows all the tricks!

The rod suddenly bends and dances.
The first fish is on the line!

They will remember this always...

Summer jobs are fun!

Crops need gathering –
line up the best ones with care.

Ducklings need to be counted –
but don't touch!

Summer games are hot and humid.

The innings pass by slowly.

Tape up a glove, play with the sand –
when are we up again?

Summer boys dream of glory,
calling the shot in the classic style.

Heart pounding, dust in mouth,
time stands still.

Summer twilights are pure magic.

Bright lights and carousel music
draw families together.

First gallop on a tall white pony…
Ride away on your dreams.

29

Summer memories never fade.

The best times will last forever,

to be remembered year after year,

when you share them with someone you love.

ART WORK BY TITLE

Artwork available at: www.john-newby.com, toll free 1-877-239-5671, fine galleries throughout North America or visit the John Newby Gallery 450 Queenston Road, R.R.#4, Niagara-on-the-Lake, Ontario, L0S 1J0.